Martin John Spalding

Pastoral Letter of the Most Rev. Martin John Spalding

Archbishop of Baltimore to the Clergy and Laity of the Archdiocese

Promulgating the Jubilee

Martin John Spalding

Pastoral Letter of the Most Rev. Martin John Spalding
Archbishop of Baltimore to the Clergy and Laity of the Archdiocese Promulgating the Jubilee

ISBN/EAN: 9783337032104

Printed in Europe, USA, Canada, Australia, Japan

Cover: Foto ©Andreas Hilbeck / pixelio.de

More available books at **www.hansebooks.com**

PASTORAL LETTER

OF THE

MOST REV. MARTIN JOHN SPALDING, D. D.

ARCHBISHOP OF BALTIMORE,

TO THE CLERGY AND LAITY OF THE ARCHDIOCESE;

PROMULGATING THE JUBILEE.

BALTIMORE:
PRINTED AND PUBLISHED BY KELLY & PIET,
OFFICE OF THE "CATHOLIC MIRROR,"
No. 174 BALTIMORE STREET.
1865.

PASTORAL LETTER

OF THE

MOST REV. MARTIN JOHN SPALDING, D. D.

ARCHBISHOP OF BALTIMORE,

TO THE CLERGY AND LAITY OF THE ARCHDIOCESE,

PROMULGATING THE JUBILEE.

Venerable Brethren of the Clergy:
Beloved Brethren of the Laity :—

IN the first Pastoral Letters, which duty requires Us to address to you, it is Our happy privilege to be the bearer of good tidings of great joy. Our venerated and beloved Chief Pastor, Pius IX., has again opened the treasury of the Church to all the faithful of Christendom, and proclaimed a solemn Jubilee of thanksgiving and supplication.

I.—JUBILEES UNDER PIUS IX.

This is the fifth Jubilee which he has announced, during his eventful Pontificate of nineteen years. The first was one of joy, on the occasion of his auspicious election to fill the Chair of Peter, in 1846 ; the second was in 1850, the regular period for the Jubilee, and it was one partly of joy for his return from exile at Gaeta, and partly of sorrow for the terrible ravages made by a bloody and uncalled for revolution, which had driven him from his See ; the third— in 1854—was one of united supplication, to implore the light of heaven to guide him in the momentous question of authoritatively defining the doctrine of the Immaculate Conception ; the fourth—in 1858—was inspired by the holy joy which overflowed his paternal heart, after he had witnessed the devoted loyalty of his people during a triumphant progress he had made through a portion of his States—since snatched from him, alas! by the rapacious violence of a neighbor powerful as he was unscrupulous; and the fifth is that now proclaimed, to awaken the attention of all Christendom to the torrent of pestilent errors, which are now prevailing, and threatening to overwhelm the Church, and along with it, all civil society; and to unite all the faithful followers of Christ in one general and earnest supplication to God, that He would mercifully interpose to control the storm, and avert the impending danger.

II.—The Immortality of the Church.

Civil society may be subverted and may fall into anarchy and ruin, for civil society is but human; but the Church is divine and immortal; built on a rock by a divine Architect, it is guarantied from destruction by His infallible promise, that "the gates of hell shall not prevail against it." The passions of the wicked and the powerful may be unchained against it, and their evil machinations may appear for a time to be on the point of compassing its destruction; their shouts of anticipated triumph may even ring through the world; but, in the end, they are themselves dashed to pieces against that rock, which has stood firm and unshaken amidst the storms of eighteen centuries, and their premature boasting is sure to be turned into the humiliation and confusion of defeat. It has been so for eighteen hundred years; it will be so, "all days, even to the consummation of the world!" He who built this everlasting Church—always "doomed to death, but ever fated not to die"—has said: "Heaven and earth may pass away, but My word shall not pass away." "Why," then, "have the gentiles raged and the people devised vain things? The kings of the earth stood up, and the princes met together, against the Lord, and against His Christ. Let us break their bonds asunder; and let us cast away their yoke from us. He that dwelleth in heaven shall laugh at them, and the Lord shall laugh them to scorn!" (Psalm ii., 1—4.)

III.—ATTITUDE OF THE PONTIFF.

Amidst the fearful tempest which now threatens with shipwreck the feeble bark of Peter, the attitude of the humble Successor of the Fisherman is calm, collected, imperturbable, verging even on the sublime! It is the living embodiment of moral power clad in the panoply of heaven, contending hopefully and heroically against overwhelming physical force, armed with all the terrible appliances of modern warfare. A feeble old man, the weakest of all the sovereigns of Europe, despoiled by brute force of the better and richer portion of the small domain which had descended to him in peaceful and unquestioned succession for more than a thousand years, and which he held in sacred trust for the benefit of all Christendom; his status determined, and his possessions—or rather those of the Church—bartered away by diplomatic negotiations and conventions, coolly entered into without either his participation or consent, by powerful neighbors calling themselves children of the Church; brought to bay, at length, by the approaching crisis in his affairs, is he cast down, is he overwhelmed? No; but he rises buoyantly on the wave which threatens to ingulph him, and elevating himself to the full height of the emergency, he dares proclaim to emperors, kings, and peoples great truths and principles, which they appear to have forgotten, which it was not pleasant for them to hear, but which it was his duty to utter. With calm dignity becoming his station, he alludes not directly to his own particular grievances, but he takes in, at a glance, the evil principles and influences which . threaten the subversion of all Society and of all Religion; and he boldly proclaims, that might does not consecrate right, that God and His Church are not to be banished with impunity from the government of the world, that human legislation is not to overbear divine principles and institutions, and that infidelity and radicalism will destroy, while Religion alone can save human society from the deluge of evils which threatens its disorganization.

IV.—Defense of the Encyclical.

That this is the main drift and real import of the weighty
Encyclical which has so startled the world, will sufficiently
appear to every reflecting and impartial man from its careful
perusal. The howl of indignation with which the world
has received the document only proves, that the healing shaft
has reached the ulcer which has so long threatened the very
life of modern society ; while the pains taken by the English
press—from which a great portion of the American has
copied—to mutilate and disfigure its meaning through a
faulty translation, seems to indicate an instinctive dread,
lest, if faithfully rendered, it might bear too forcibly on
evils, which are the more fondly cherished, because they are
flattering to the pride of the human heart, and have already
become well nigh inveterate. It was to be expected that the
world would be indignant, when it was thus suddenly
awakened from its dream of an earthly Elysium, amid the
wonderful modern developments of material comforts and
interests, by the voice of a venerable man who dared tell its
votaries, in the name of God, whose chief minister he is on
earth, that "all is vanity," that "the figure of this world
passeth away," and that the great end of our creation is not
to accumulate wealth, but to lay up treasures in heaven, and
to labor for eternity ; but the verdict of the world is evidently much too interested and self-seeking, to possess any
real weight with those upon whose souls the blessed light of
revelation has dawned, and who, through God's teaching,
·have happily learned to estimate at their real value the
baubles which men prize most, and through the inordinate
love of which they peril their immortal souls, selling their
birth-right to heaven for a mess of earthly pottage ! "WHAT
DOTH IT PROFIT A MAN, IF HE GAIN THE WHOLE WORLD, AND
LOSE HIS OWN SOUL?" "O sons of men, how long will ye be
dull of heart? Why do ye love vanity, and seek after
lying." (Psalm iv. 3.)

A few extracts from the Encyclical will establish the accu-
racy of Our interpretation of its real purport and meaning.

The intrepid Pontiff unites with his Predecessors in warning the faithful against " the machinations of those evil men who, ' foaming out their own confusion, like the raging waves of the sea,' and promising liberty while they themselves are the slaves of corruption, have endeavored, by their fallacious opinions and most wicked writings, to subvert the foundations of the Catholic Religion and of civil Society, to remove from our midst all virtue and justice, to deprave the minds and hearts of all, to turn away from the right discipline of morals the incautious, and especially inexperienced youth, miserably corrupting them, leading them into the nets of error, and finally withdrawing them from the bosom of the Church." (P. 2, *Official copy*.)

Who these wicked men are, who thus machinate, the Pontiff sufficiently declares in the following passage : " For you know well, Venerable Brethren, that at this time there are found not a few, who applying to civil intercourse (*consortio*) the impious and absurd principle of what they call *Naturalism*, dare teach, that the best form (*ratio*) of society, and the exigencies of civil progress absolutely require human society to be constituted and governed *without any regard whatever to Religion, as if this did not even exist,* or at least without making any distinction between true and false religions." (P. 4.)

The men who advocate this, as the best theory of human society, are evidently not only latitudinarians, but downright infidels, who believe in *Naturalism* as opposed to *Supernaturalism*, in *reason* as opposed to *Revelation*, in man as opposed to God. And these same unscrupulous and impious men very naturally extend their theory of social optimism, so as to shield from just punishment " the violators of the Catholic Religion, unless in so far as the public peace may require." They very consistently advocate, "as the best condition of society," that in which they can at will rob the Catholic Church of its property, and violate all its time consecrated rights, provided they can do so with impunity, and without violating " the public peace !"

The idea of the Pontiff is still further illustrated in the following passage, in which he refers to the cherished error of these same *Naturalists*, who, impatient of all restraint, whether human or divine, seek to banish God and His eternal truth and justice from human society :—

"And since Religion has been excluded from civil society, and the doctrine and authority of divine Revelation repudiated, or the true and germane notion of justice and human right obscured and lost, and material or brute force substituted in the place of true justice and legitimate right, it is easy to perceive why some persons, forgetting and trampling upon the most certain principles of sound reason, dare cry out together, 'that the will of the people, manifested by what they call public opinion, or in any other way, constitutes the the supreme law, *independent of all divine and human right*, and that, in the political order, *consummated facts, by the very fact that they are consummated, have the force of right.'* But who does not see and plainly understand, that the society of men, freed from the bonds of Religion and true justice, can certainly have no other purpose than the effort to obtain and accumulate wealth, and that in its actions it follows no other law than that of the uncurbed cupidity which seeks to secure its own pleasures and comforts?" (P. 6.)

He goes on portraying these wicked men, whom he designates successively, Naturalists, Socialists, and Communists, setting forth their inveterate hatred of Religious Families (Conventual Establishments), whose rich possessions, so long devoted to the purposes of charity and learning, they ardently covet ; their opposition to generous Catholic charity, evidenced by their openly announced wish, " that citizens and the Church should be deprived of the privilege of openly bestowing alms for the sake of charity ;" and their manifest hatred of all Religion, exhibited in their desire to see abolished the wise Christian law, " by which, to afford facilities for the worship of God, servile works are prohibited on certain days ;" finally, their favorite theory, " that domestic society, or the family, derives *from the civil law alone all its rights of existence*, and that consequently, *all the right of parents over their children*, and particularly the right of instruction and education, flows from and depends upon *the civil law alone.*" (Pp. 6 and 7.)

In the light of these declarations, openly and persistently made by the self-styled Liberals—but really infidels—of Europe, it is easy to understand what is contained in the Encyclical, in condemnation of the assertion by them, "that the liberty of conscience and of worship is the peculiar (inalienable) right of every man, which should be proclaimed by law, and asserted in every well constituted society, and that citizens have the right *to all kinds of liberty (omnimodam libertatem), to be restrained by no law, whether ecclesiastical or civil*, by which they may be enabled to manifest openly and publicly their ideas (*conceptus*) by word of mouth, through the press, or by any other means." This species of lawless liberty he rightly designates, with the great St. Augustine, "the liberty of perdition." To the extent to which it is maintained by the European infidels, it amounts, in fact, to anarchy and Jacobinism in politics, and to radicalism, rationalism, and infidelity in Religion. These European Liberals are so enamored of liberty, as to desire its monopoly for themselves ; they wish to enjoy it all, without allowing any of its privileges to their neighbors. While they claim the freedom to attack the most cherished institutions of Religion and Society, unrestrained by any law, human or divine, those whom they assail are to be denounced as friends of despotism, if they dare open their mouths in legitimate self-defence !

Is it not fair and equitable, Venerable and Beloved Brethren, to understand in this sense only the solemn denunciation of the Pontiff? Is it not a sound canon of interpretation, to seek the meaning of a declaration, particularly if it be a solemn and official one, in the context and the circumstances which called it forth? Is it not evident, from the mere reading of the Encyclical, that the liberty of conscience and of worship is condemned only in the sense, in which it was asserted by its latitudinarian and infidel champions? These maintain it, on the ground that all religions are alike and equal *before God*, as well as before men, and that they are all alike superstitious and false, good enough perhaps for nervous old women and feeble-minded children, but totally unworthy the attention of strong-minded men! This is surely rather *license* than *liberty;* it is infidelity rather than Religion. Every true lover of Christ and of His holy Religion should then cheerfully unite, heart and soul, with the Pontiff, in placing upon such liberty as this the stigma of solemn condemnation. "Oh liberty! How many crimes are not committed in thy name."

V.—OUR OWN FREE GOVERNMENT—THE SYLLABUS.

To stretch the words of the Pontiff, evidently intended for the stand-point of European radicals and infidels, so as to make them include the state of things established in this country, by our noble Constitution, in regard to the liberty of conscience, of worship, and of the press, were manifestly unfair and unjust. Divided as we were in religious sentiment from the very origin of our government, our fathers acted most prudently and wisely in adopting as an Amendment to the Constitution, the organic law, that "Congress shall make no law respecting the establishment of Religion, or prohibiting the free exercise thereof." (Amend 1.) In fact, under the circumstances, they could have adopted no other course, consistently with the principles and even with the very existence of our newly established government.

In adopting this Amendment, they certainly did not intend, like the European radicals, disciples of Tom Paine and of the French Revolution, to pronounce all religions, whether true or false, equal before God, but only to declare them equal before the law ; or rather, simply to lay down the sound and equitable principle, that the civil government, adhering strictly to its own appropriate sphere of political duty, pledged itself not to interfere with religious matters, which it rightly viewed as entirely without the bounds of its competency. The founders of our government were, thank God, neither Latitudinarians nor infidels ; they were earnest, honest men ; and however much some of them may have been personally lukewarm in the matter of Religion, or may have differed in religious opinions, they still professed to believe in Christ and His Revelatio*, and exhibited a commendable respect for religious observances. Therefore their action could not have been condemned, or even contemplated, by the Pontiff, in his recent solemn censure, pronounced on an altogether different set of men with a totally different set of principles—on men and on principles so very clearly and emphatically portrayed in the document itself, which every sound canon of interpretation requires to be strictly construed.

All other matters contained in the Encyclical, as well as the long catalogue of eighty propositions condemned in its appendix, or *Syllabus*, are to be judged of by the same standard. These propositions are condemned in the sense of those who uttered and maintained them, and in no other. To be fair in our interpretation, we must never lose sight of the lofty stand-point of the Pontiff, who steps forth as the champion of law and order, against anarchy and revolution, and of revealed Religion against more or less openly avowed infidelity ; nor should we forget the stand-point of those whose errors he condemns, who openly or covertly assail all revealed Religion, and seek to sap the very foundations of all well-ordered society ; who threaten to bring back into the world the untold horrors of the French Revolution, and to make the streets and the highways run with the blood of the best and noblest citizens. Their covert attacks against Religion and Society are, perhaps, even more formidable than their open assaults. Against the latter, the virtuous are readily guarded and armed ; against the former, which often bear the appearance of good, and whose evil drift is not so easily perceived, we are are not so well prepared, and the poison of error is often insidiously instilled into the minds and hearts of the well-disposed but simple-minded, before they even think of guarding against danger, or seasonably applying the antidote.

And this naturally leads us to another remark, the justice and fairness of which will be apparent to every right-minded thinker. It is this. Propositions condemned *in globo*, like those in the *Syllabus*, are intended to receive different measures of censure, according to their intrinsic nature and their extrinsic bearings : some are censured much more mildly than others; and some even more from the too general or dangerous interpretation of which they are susceptible, or which they have actually received from their authors, than from intrinsic reasons founded upon the strict construction of the text itself, apart from its surroundings. All who are familiar with the course usually adopted by the Holy See, in condemning thus *in globo* whole series of propositions extracted from the writings of suspected or heretical authors, will discover, at a glance, the equity and justice of this statement.

Those who are so indignant at the plain speaking of the Papal denunciation, would do well to reserve a portion of their anger for the inspired Apostle of the gentiles, who stigmatizes error and vice with at least equal point and boldness. In the following passage, he graphically portrays the pernicious errors and the glaring wickedness of these very "last days" upon which we are so sadly fallen ;— every epithet in it is a picture drawn from life, and the whole is a word-painting of marvellous truth and power ; prophecy revealing the mystery of iniquity, "which is now working," to his eagle glance, and inspiration pointing his pen :—

"Know this also, that in the last days dangerous times shall come : men will be lovers of self, covetous, boastful, haughty, blasphemous, disobedient to parents, ungrateful, wicked ; without affection, without peace, slanderers, incontinent, cruel, unkind ; traitors, headstrong, puffed up, and lovers of pleasure more than of God : having indeed an appearance of piety, but denying the power thereof ; * * * *always learning and never attaining to the knowledge of the truth.* But as Jannes and Mambres resisted Moses, so these also resist the truth, men corrupted in mind, reprobate concerning the faith. But they shall not advance further ; for their folly will be manifest to all, as theirs was also." (II. Timothy iii. 1 seq.)

VI.—CHARACTER OF PIUS IX.

All impartial men, Venerable and Beloved Brethren, who are acquainted with the mild and amiable character, and with the eventful and almost romantic history of our venerated and beloved Pius IX., will be slow to judge harshly of anything he has ever said, written, or done. Taken from the bosom of the people who so loved him, though himself of noble lineage, he was raised to the Pontificate amidst the acclamations of the people. He at once threw himself into their arms, and, first of all European sovereigns, he inaugurated free institutions far in advance of the times, as the event proved. He proclaimed a general Amnesty, brought back the political exiles, and, amidst the congratulations of Europe and America, he granted and proclaimed a liberal Constitution to his people, whose idol he at once became.

The scene soon changes, and what was so auspiciously begun and so generously granted, soon terminates disastrously, and the glory of the new Pontiff-King speedily sets in blood, not shed by him—for he never shed any one's blood—but shed by those very men, whose signal benefactor he had been, and who now, in return, repay his goodness with ungrateful treachery and bloody machinations against his throne and his very life. His prime minister is assassinated at the very opening of the chambers under the Constitution ; the bloody dagger is paraded in triumph through the streets of the eternal city ; the so lately idolized Pontiff is besieged in his own palace by a mob goaded to fury by the conspirators, and the ball, which was probably intended for him, strikes down at his side his amiable and learned private secretary, Dr. Palma ; he escapes himself at length in disguise, and he becomes an exile at Gaeta, where the world loves and reverences him in his fallen fortunes, more even, perhaps, than it had done when he was dwelling in the splendid palaces of his Predecessors. His divine Lord and Master was insulted and crucified by the people among whom he had gone about doing good ; and it was meet that the disciple should not be above the Master.

14

Restored at length to his See, amidst the acclamations of Christendom, he has for the last fifteen years been encompassed with difficulties such as had fallen to the lot of few among his Predecessors in modern times, of none probably, if we except the two Sainted men who bore his name—Pius VI. and Pius VII. Beset with political machinations from without and with conspiracies from within, he has been always like a lamb in the midst of wolves ; a lamb in meekness, but a lion in courage. He has put his trust in God, and he has not been confounded. He has clothed himself with the armor of God, and he has proved invulnerable to all the fiery shafts of the evil one. With St. Paul he could say with truth : "For the weapons of our warfare are not carnal, but mighty unto God, for the destruction of fortresses, destroying counsels, and every height that exalteth itself against the knowledge of God, and bringing into captivity every understanding to the obedience of Christ." (II. Corinthians, x. 4, seq.) He has ever conquered, and he will yet conquer, by wielding only the sword of the spirit, which is the word of life. His words are even now far more powerful than the mighty weapons of his adversaries. He speaks in the name of Christ, and Christendom receives his words with reverence and with love ; even his enemies are startled at their utterance, and they tremble amidst the clamorous indignation to which they give expression, apparently to drown their apprehensions. They seem to feel instinctively, that there is, after all, something mysteriously impressive, and approaching at once the sublime and the divine, in the declarations of that feeble old man who sits in the Vatican.

His warning against the errors of the times forcibly remind Us, Venerable and Beloved Brethren, of those uttered by the first Apostle Pontiff, whose Successor he is : " Even as there shall be among you false teachers, who will bring in sects of perdition, and denying the Lord who bought them, bring on themselves swift destruction ; and many shall follow their excesses, through whom the way of truth shall be dishonored ; and through covetousness, *with feigned words, will make merchandize of you."* (II. Peter, 11. 1 seq.) In the language of the same chief Apostle, his present Successor warns all the lovers of true liberty to be "as free, and not having liberty as a cloak of maliciousness, but as servants of God;" (II. Peter, ii., 16) and in that of the divine Master Himself: "And ye will know the truth, and the truth shall make you free." (St. John viii. 32).

VII. TEMPORAL POWER OF THE POPE.

It is not, indeed, an article of the Catholic faith that the Pope should be an earthly Sovereign ; his Primacy is independent of his temporal power. His spiritual authority, derived from Christ through St. Peter, is divine and immortal, and it would be as much respected were he a persecuted exile, as have been many of his Predecessors, as it is while he occupies his normal position at the Vatican. Still his temporal Sovereignty, rendering him, as it does independent of all other governments, is a most useful appendage to the Primacy, the free exercise of which it secures and guaranties ; and it is, moreover, the most legitimate Sovereignty on the earth, created more than a thousand years ago on the spontaneous and urgent call of the people themselves, abandoned by the Greek emperors to the incursions of the Northern Barbarians. And any Catholic who would question the wisdom of this providential arrangement, which has proved so beneficial in the long lapse of ages, would be justly deemed guilty of imprudence and rashness ; while those who would seek to disturb it by violence, would be subject to the anathema denounced against the violators of Church property. The fathers of our own country wisely ordained that the National Government should be located in a territory independent of State jurisdiction, thus imitating, in our political organization, the wise provision which God's Providence had already made, in order to secure the independent action of the central authority and general government of His Church.

If the Pontiff is so much embarrassed in his intercourse with the Catholic world, as it is, what would be his condition, were he the subject of any one among the European powers? Would Victor Emmanuel allow him free intercourse with Austria; would any Catholic government receive his communications, even on purely spiritual subjects, if made by him as the subject of a power with which it was at war? Would it, in this case, have been possible for him, for example, to issue the present Encyclical, or in fact, any other document of an official character, warning the faithful against the errors and immoralities of the age? Would he be permitted to tell unpalatable truths to his own Sovereign, or to any other? In ceasing to be an independent sovereign, he would become the veriest slave. He would be hampered and thwarted at every step, and the exercise of his Spiritual Primacy would become exceedingly difficult, if not wholly impossible. As it is, he has—or rather had—just territory enough to support him and his necessary officials modestly, according to his station; not enough to give him any preponderating influence in political affairs. He is, at the same time, the weakest and the most powerful Sovereign in Christendom; the weakest in physical force, the strongest in moral power.

VIII.—The Acceptable Time.

It behooves us, Venerable and Beloved Brethren, on this solemn occasion, to enter, with earnest and loving faith, into the sentiments of our beloved Chief Pastor, and to unite together in fervent supplications to God, that He may avert the storm which threatens His Church, stretching forth His all-mighty hand over the swelling waves which toss the bark of Peter, and bidding them be still!—" And we working together with Him, do exhort you, that ye receive not the grace of God in vain. For he saith, in an acceptable time I have heard thee, and in the day of salvation I have helped thee. Behold! now is the acceptable time; behold! now is the day of salvation!" (II. Corinth., vi., 1 seq.) To borrow the language of the eloquent St. John Chrysostom, " prayer is the source, is the root, is the mother of countless blessings; the power of prayer extinguishes the flames, curbs the fury of lions, suspends wars, appeases combats, calms tempests, puts the demons to flight, opens the gates of heaven, breaks the bonds of death, cures diseases, drives away misfortunes, strengthens tottering cities, averts the scourges of heaven, and defeats the attacks of men ; there are no evils which prayer does not dissipate."

IX.—NATURE OF INDULGENCES.

As you are already well informed, Venerable and Beloved Brethren, a Jubilee is the most ample form of Plenary Indulgence. You have also been fully instructed, that an Indulgence is a remission only of the temporal punishment, which often remains due to sin, after the guilt itself and the eternal punishment consequent upon it have been already remitted. It not only, then, is no pardon of sin, but it necessarily pre-supposes that the sin itself has been already pardoned, and, *in this case only*, can it take effect. Such being clearly the doctrine of the Catholic Church, we are not to heed the clamor of sectarians, who, either wholly misapprehending or grievously misstating our belief on this subject, pretend that an Indulgence is a license to commit sin, or at least an incentive to sin. Rather should we, during this holy season of prayer, pour forth earnest supplications to the Father of Lights, that He would vouchsafe to remove the scales from the eyes of those erring brethren, many of whom, through blindness and an evil education, seem always ready to believe everything but the truth, as it is in Christ Jesus.

An Indulgence can surely be no incentive to sin, since it can take no effect whatever in the soul until the sin has been previously forgiven, by the merits of the blood of Christ, applied through the sacrament of Penance. To obtain this forgiveness, the Catholic Church requires not only *all* the conditions which the sects usually assign, such as faith and sincere repentance ; but, moreover, confession to a lawfully authorized minister of Christ, and some works of satisfaction and mortification, deriving their supernatural value and efficacy, for appeasing God's justice, from their union with the abounding merits and sufferings of Christ.

By denying this Catholic doctrine of satisfaction, which is the very basis of Indulgences ; and the logical sequel to it, —that after the remission of sin, some temporal punishment often remains due to God's rigorous justice, to be undergone either in this world or in the expiating flames of Purgatory in the next,—our dissenting brethren really grant to their followers a standing plenary Indulgence of the most ample kind, and on the lightest possible conditions ! If there be, then, any encouragement of sin, it is not certainly the Catholic Church, but the sects opposed to her, who are guilty of it, by removing from repentance all those things which are hardest to flesh and blood, and making the conditions of pardon so very light and easy.

X.—THE JEWISH AND THE CHRISTIAN JUBILEE.

A Jubilee is, as We have said, the most solemn and the most ample form of plenary Indulgence. It is an application to the soul of the truly contrite and already *forgiven* sinner of the most abundant treasures of the Church, based upon the unlimited power of the Keys and of binding and loosing, imparted by Christ to St. Peter and to his Successors in the Apostolic office. Only the generous and the fervent Christian can hope to share, to the full, in these exuberant riches of the divine mercy ; but to such, the Jubilee is really, what its name implies, a season of gladness and of joy unspeakable. These fervent souls hear with exultation the words of the Lord : "Sound the trumpet, and proclaim remission to all the inhabitants of thy land ; for it is the year of Jubilee." (Leviticus, xxv.)

Under the Mosaic dispensation, the Jubilee was celebrated with joyful and solemn observances every fiftieth year. The land lay fallow ; the vines were left unpruned ; and whatever grew spontaneously on the soil was held to be common to masters and servants, to strangers and natives, to animals and men. All debts were forgiven ; those who had been compelled to sell or alienate their possessions were restored

19

to their inheritance; the trammels of the bondsman were loosed, and he was permitted to return in joyful freedom to his family.

Such were the beneficent provisions made by God Himself for the Jewish Jubilee. They looked, indeed, mainly to the temporal order, but they were well calculated to wean the hearts of the chosen people of the olden time from the perishing things of this world, and to turn them to God, upon whose bountiful and never-failing Providence all were made wholly to depend for subsistence every fiftieth year. The Jewish life thus moved in cycles of fifty years; at the close of each of which, there was a solemn pause, or *Sabbath*—a year of rest and remission—during which all were to repose from their cares and labors, and to turn with their whole hearts to the Lord their God.

It was a beautiful dispensation; yet withal as inferior to ours, as is the type to the prototype, the shadow to the reality; or, in other words, as is Judaism, with its imposing "shadow of the good things to come," to the vivid, life-giving, and splendid realities of Christianity. The Christian Jubilee is the fulfilment and realization of the Jewish. Its provisions contemplate the spiritual order, the relations of man to God and to eternity. The freedom which it promises, is that from the galling bondage of sin, it is "the liberty of the glory of the children of God." The rich inheritance to which it offers to restore us, is that of God's superabounding grace here on earth, and of His glorious and eternal Kingdom hereafter in heaven: where "eye hath not seen, nor ear heard, nor hath it entered into the heart of man (to conceive,) what good things God hath prepared for them that love Him." It causeth the exuberant soil of the Church spontaneously to germinate, and to produce in abundance the richest plants of virtue and holiness, for the healing of the nations. Truly, then, We repeat, "now is the acceptable time, now is the day of salvation." Two hundred millions of Christians, of all nations and peoples and tongues, united in prayer! Only the Catholic Church can present a spectacle so sublime as this!

The Christian Jubilee was originally estabished, with a view to its taking place every hundred years, at the commencement of the century. The Bull of Pope Boniface VIII., issued in 1300, appears to be the first authentic record of the Jubilee in its present form. The number of pious pilgrims, who, in that year, flocked to Rome to gain the Indulgence, appears almost incredible, in our cold, calculating age of Mammon-worship. During no part of that year, was the number of such pilgrims estimated at less than two hundred thousand.

To gratify the fervent piety of the faithful, the period was subsequently reduced to fifty years, in imitation of the Jewish Jubilee, by Pope Clement VI., towards the middle of the fourteenth century. This discipline continued for about a century—till the year 1450—the last occasion on which the fifty years' Jubilee was celebrated. Pope Paul II., stimulated by the ever-increasing devotion of the faithful, in a Bull issued in 1470, reduced the period to twenty-five years, a practice which has been maintained to the present day. In addition, however, to the stated Jubilees recurring every quarter of a century, subsequent Pontiffs have adopted the custom of publishing an extraordinary Jubilee on their accession to the chair of Peter, and on occasions of great public calamities, or of special exigencies of the times, which, in their judgment seemed to call for this union of prayers among the faithful throughout Christendom.

XI.—OUR IMMACULATE MOTHER IN HEAVEN.

It is not without significance, Venerable and Beloved Brethren, that the Encyclical Letters of the Holy Father were dated on the Feast of the Immaculate Conception of the Blessed Virgin, and on the tenth anniversary of the solemn definition of this great privilege, which the pious belief of ages had awarded to Mary. Every believer in the divinity of Jesus, as God in the Flesh, and every one who loves Jesus, and dearly prizes the high honor of claiming Him as a Brother, must necessarily feel a tender filial reverence for His Mother, who, by the very fact of the Incarnation, becomes *our* Mother as well. Bequeathed to the Beloved Disciple' as a Mother by Jesus, with his expiring breath, she is loved as such by all, who like John, seek to be the favorites of Jesus. It has been so from the very beginning of the Church; it will be so to the end of time. What a privilege to have a Mother in heaven; and so tender, so powerful, and so sweet a Mother! Christ, who denied her nothing on earth, will surely deny her nothing in heaven! Whatever we ask through Mary, with earnest and persevering faith, we shall most certainly obtain, if it be conducive to our salvation. Let us, then, during these days of benediction, implore her powerful intercession for ourselves, for those dear to us, and for the holy Church for which her Son died on the cross. Our faith and devotion should be stimulated by the fact, that she is the chosen Patroness of our beloved country, for the welfare and prosperity of which, both temporal and spiritual, she will not fail to raise her Immaculate hands before the throne of her divine Son. She is also the principal Patroness of this Archdiocese, and the first town of the Colony was called after her by our pious ancestors. She will not, cannot forget the *land* which bears her own sweet name.

XII. Conditions for Gaining the Jubilee Indulgence.

The Pontiff having authorized Us to designate any month within the year 1865, for obtaining the Indulgence of the present Jubilee, and having also made it Our duty to designate the Churches to be visited and other works to be performed, in accordance with his Bull issued November 20, 1846 ; We hereby appoint, for this Archdiocese, the month beginning on the first Sunday of Lent, March 5th, and ending on the Tuesday after Passion Sunday, April 4th, both these days being included. We also designate, as the Churches to be visited, the following : for Baltimore, the Cathedral, St. Vincent's, and St. Michael's ; for Washington and Georgetown, St. Patrick's, St. Matthew's and the Holy Trinity ; for all the other portions of the Archdiocese, the parochial Church, or the Chapel in convents, colleges, academias, and in country places, where the Holy Sacrifice is usually offered up for the people.

One visit to all the three Churches above named, or two visits to any one of them, or to one of the others mentioned above, with prayers offered up at each visit, according to the intentions of the Sovereign Pontiff, "for some space of time," will be required as a condition for gaining the Indulgence. These intentions are: 1st, the preservation and protection of the Pontiff himself; 2d, the extension of the faith, and the prosperity of the Holy Catholic Church : 3d, the conversion of sinners and of those in error; 4th, peace among Christian princes, rulers, and peoples. No particular form of prayer is prescribed, but for those who cannot conveniently read the prayers indicated in the small Manual for the Jubilee, the fervent recitation of five Our Fathers and five Hail Marys will suffice. The other conditions for gaining the Indulgence are the following :—

1. A good confession and communion ; but for children who have not made their first communion, and who cannot be conveniently prepared for it, a good confession with absolution will be sufficient.

.2 Fasting on Wednesday, Friday, and Saturday of one week during the month assigned. Those who are unable to fast, may have this condition commuted by their confessor into some other good work.

3. The bestowal of some alms on the poor, "as each one's devotion may suggest." This condition may also be commuted by the confessor in favor of the poor, while in religious houses the superior may bestow the alms for the entire community, and in families parents for their children and servants.

It is Our wish, that the alms thus collected throughout the Archdiocese be divided by the respective Pastors into two equal parts, one of which he will apply to local charities, and the other he will remit to Our Secretary, to constitute the beginning of a fund for erecting a Diocesan Reformatory for Boys near Baltimore, a charity very much needed, if we would save our poor children, in body and in soul.

In favor of the sick, of travelers, of soldiers, of those in prison, and of all others legitimately prevented from complying with the conditions for gaining the Indulgence during the month above designated, We hereby extend the time to any period within the year 1865, which their Pastor or Spiritual Director may appoint.

And We also hereby authorize the Pastors of Churches outside the cities of Baltimore and Washington, to appoint any other month within the year than that above indicated, if, in their judgment, it would be for the spiritual benefit of their flock; provided, that for each such change, they have Our express approbation, that the appointed month do not interfere with the Retreat of the Clergy, which will open in Baltimore, at the Seminary of St. Sulpice, on the 16th of May, and that they do not select a time inconvenient to the people in the agricultural districts.

Those having care of souls will impress on their people the necessity of complying strictly with *all* the conditions for gaining the Indulgence; and they will also be careful to state that, while fasting for three days during Lent will suffice, the Paschal Communion, which is of strict obligation on all, will not fulfil the condition of the communion requisite for the Jubilee.

Pastors of the various congregations are requested so to arrange the particular time for the exercises in their respective Churches, as to be able to assist one another, so far as circumstances may permit. It is desirable, that these exercises, to be determined by each Pastor, should continue for at least one week in the larger congregations, and for three days in the smaller. A solemn mission will be opened in Our Cathedral on the second Sunday of Lent, and it will continue for two weeks, till the fourth Sunday inclusive.

This Pastoral Letter will be read in all the Churches on occasion of opening the Jubilee, or on the Sunday preceding, at the option of the Pastors.

And now, Venerable and Beloved Brethren, We commend Ourselves and this Archdiocese, to the government of which We have been called in the Providence of God, to your fervent prayers, during this season of grace and benediction.

The grace of Our Lord Jesus Christ be with you all. Amen.

Given from Our residence in Baltimore on the Feast of St. John of Matha, February 8th, in the year of Our Lord 1865.

MARTIN JOHN SPALDING,
Archbishop of Baltimore.

THOMAS FOLEY, *Secretary.*

☞ As several imperfect or faulty English translations of the Encyclical Letter of the Pope, and of its Annex, or *Syllabus* of errors condemned, have been published, it has been thought expedient to republish both documents, in a version which has been carefully revised and compared with the original, and which may therefore be regarded as substantially correct and authentic.

THE ENCYCLICAL OF POPE PIUS IX.

PIUS PP. IX.

To Our Venerable Brothers, the Patriarchs, Primates, Archbishops, and Bishops, of the Universal Church, having Grace and Communion with the Apostolic See.

HEALTH AND APOSTOLIC BENEDICTION :

It is well known unto all men, and especially to You, Venerable Brothers, with what great care and pastoral vigilance Our Predecessors, the Roman Pontiffs, have discharged the Office entrusted by Christ Our Lord to them, in the Person of the Most Blessed Peter, Prince of the Apostles, have unremittingly discharged the duty of feeding the lambs and the sheep, and have diligently nourished the Lord's entire flock with the words of faith, imbued it with salutary doctrine, and guarded it from poisoned pastures. And those Our Predecessors, who were the assertors and Champions of the august Catholic Religion, of truth and justice, being as they were chiefly solicitous for the salvation of souls, held nothing to be of so great importance as the duty of exposing and condemning, in their most wise Letters and Constitutions, all heresies and errors which are hostile to moral honesty and to the eternal salvation of mankind, and which have frequently stirred up terrible commotions and have damaged both the Christian and civil commonwealths in a disastrous manner. Wherefore those Our Predecessors have, with Apostolic fortitude continually resisted the machinations of those evil men, who, "foaming out their own confusion, like the raging waves of the sea," and "promising liberty, while they are themselves the slaves of corruption," endeavored by their fallacious opinions and most wicked writings to subvert the foundations of Religion and of civil Society, to remove from our midst all virtue and justice, to deprave the hearts and minds of all, to turn away from right discipline of morals the incautious, and especially inexperienced youth, miserably corrupting them, leading them into the nets of error, and finally withdrawing them from the bosom of the Catholic Church.

And now, Venerable Brothers, as is also very well known to you, scarcely had We (by the secret dispensation of Divine Providence, certainly by no merit of Our own) been called to this Chair of Peter, when We, to the extreme grief of Our soul, beheld a horrible tempest stirred· up by so many erroneous opinions, and the dreadful and never-enough to be lamented mischiefs which redound to Christian people from such errors; and We then, in discharge of Our Apostolic Ministerial Office, imitating the example of Our illustrious Predecessors, raised Our voice, and in several published Encyclical Letters, and in Allocutions delivered in Consistory, and in other Apostolical Letters, We condemned the prominent, most grievous errors of the age, and We stirred up your excellent episcopal vigilance, and again and again did We admonish and exhort all the sons of the Catholic Church, who are most dear to Us, that they should abhor and shun all the said errors, as they would the contagion of a fatal pestilence.— Especially in Our first Encyclical Letter, written to You on the 9th of November, A. D. 1846, and in two Allocutions, one of which was delivered by Us in Consistory on tHe 9th of December, A. D. 1854, and the other on the 9th of June, A. D. 1862, We condemned the monstrous and portentous opinions, which prevail especially in the present age, to the very great loss of souls, and even to the detriment of civil society; and which are in the highest degree hostile, not only to the Catholic Church, and to her salutary doctrine and venerable laws, but also to the everlasting law of nature engraven by God upon the hearts of all men, and to right reason; and out of which almost all errors originate.

Now although hitherto We have not omitted to denounce and reprove the chief errors of this kind, yet the cause of the Catholic Church and the salvation of souls committed to Us by God, and even the interests of human society absolutely demand, that once again We should stir up Your pastoral solicitude, to drive away other erroneous opinions which flow from those errors above specified, as their source. These false and perverse opinions are so much the more detestable, by as much as they have chiefly for their object to hinder and banish that salutary influence which the Catholic Church, by the institution

and command of her Divine Author, ought freely to exercise, even to
the consummation of the world, not only over individual men, but nations, peoples, and sovereigns, and to abolish that mutual co-operation
and agreement of counsels between the Priesthood and Governments,
which has always been propitious and conducive to the welfare both
of Church and State. (Gregory XVI. Encyclical, 13th August,
1832.) For you know well, Venerable Brethren, that at this time
there are found not a few, who applying to civil intercourse the impious and absurd principles of what they call *Naturalism*, dare teach,
"that the best form of Society, and the exigencies of civil progress
absolutely require human society to be constituted and governed without any regard whatsoever to Religion, as if this (Religion) did not
even exist, or at least without making any distinction between true
and false religions." Contrary to the teaching of the Holy Scriptures,
of the Church, and of the Holy Fathers, these persons do not hesitate
to assert, that "the best condition of human society is that, wherein
no duty is recognized by the Government of correcting, by enacted
penalties, the violators of the Catholic Religion, except when the main-
tenance of the public peace requires it." From this totally false notion of social government, they fear not to uphold that erroneous opinion most pernicious to the Catholic Church, and to the salvation of
souls, which was called by Our Predecessor Gregory XVI. (lately
quoted) the insanity (deliramentum), (Encycl. 13 August, 1832):
namely, "that the liberty of conscience and of worship is the peculiar (or inalienable) right of every man, which should be proclaimed
by law, and that citizens have the right to all kinds of liberty, to be
restrained by no law, whether ecclesiastical or civil, by which they
may be enabled to manifest openly and publicly their ideas, by word
of mouth, through the press, or by any other means." But whilst
these men make these rash assertions, they do not reflect, or consider,
that they preach the liberty of perdition (St. Augustine, Epistle 105.
al. 166), and that, "if it is always free to human arguments to dis-
cuss, men will never be wanting who will dare to resist the truth,
and to rely upon the loquacity of human wisdom, when we know
from the command of Our Lord Jesus Christ, how faith and Christian
wisdom ought to avoid this most mischievous vanity." (St. Leo,
Epistle 164, al. 133, sec. 2, Boll. ed.).

And since Religion has been excluded from civil Society, and the
doctrine and authority of divine Revelation, or the true and germane
notion of justice and human right have been obscured and lost, and
material or brute force substituted in the place of true justice and

. legitimate right, it is easy to perceive why some persons, forgetting and trampling upon the most certain principles of sound reason, dare cry out together, "that the will of the people, manifested by what they call public opinion, or in any other way, constitutes the supreme law, independent of all divine and human right, and that, in the political order, accomplished facts, by the mere fact of having been accomplished, have the force of right." But who does not see and plainly understand, that the Society of man, freed from the bonds of Religion and of true justice, can certainly have no other purpose than the effort to obtain and accumulate wealth, and that in its actions it follows no other law than that of the uncurbed cupidity, which seeks to secure its own pleasures and comforts? For this reason, also, these same men persecute with such bitter hatred the Religious Orders, who have deserved so well of religion, civil Society, and Letters; they loudly declare that these Orders have no right to exist, and, in so doing, make common cause with the falsehoods of the heretics. For, as was most wisely taught by Our Predecessor of illustrious memory, Pius VI., "the abolition of Religious Orders injures the state of public profession of the Evangelical Counsels; injures a mode of life recommended by the Church, as in conformity with Apostolical doctrine; does wrong to the illustrious founders whom we venerate upon our altars, and who constituted these societies under the inspiration of God." (Epistle to Cardinal de la Rochefaucauld, March 10, 1791.)

And these same persons also impiously pretend, that citizens should be deprived of the liberty of publicly bestowing on the Church their alms for the sake of Christian charity, and that the law forbidding "servile labour on account of Divine worship" upon certain fixed days should be abolished, upon the most fallacious pretext that such liberty and such law are contrary to the principles of political economy. Not content with abolishing Religion in public Society, they desire further to banish it from families and private life. Teaching and professing those most fatal errors of Socialism and Communism, they declare, that "domestic society, or the family, derives all its reason of existence solely from civil law, whence it is to be concluded that from civil law descend and depend all the rights of parents over their children, and, above all, the right of instructing and educating them." By such impious opinions and machinations, do these most false teachers endeavour to eliminate the salutary teaching and influence of the Catholic Church from the instruction and education of youth, and miserably to infect and deprave by every pernicious error and vice the tender and pliant minds of youth. All those who endeavour to throw into

confusion both religious and political affairs, to destroy the good order
of society, and to annihilate all Divine and human rights, have always
exerted all their criminal schemes, attention, and efforts upon the manner in which they might, above all, deprave and delude unthinking
youth, as We have already shown : it is upon the corruption of youth
that they place all their hopes. Thus they never cease to attack by
every method the Clergy, both secular and regular, from whom, as
testify to us in so conspicuous a manner the most certain records of
history, such considerable benefits have been bestowed in abundance
upon Christian and Civil Society and upon the republic of Letters ;
asserting of the Clergy in general, that they are the enemies of the
useful sciences, of progress, and of civilization, and that they ought
to be deprived of all participation in the work of teaching and training
the young.

Others, reviving the depraved fictions of innovators, errors many
times condemned, presume, with extraordinary impudence, to subord-
inate the authority of the Church and of this Apostolic See, conferred
upon it by Christ Our Lord, to the judgment of civil authority, and
to deny all the rights of this same Church and this See with regard to
those things which appertain to the secular order. For these persons
do not blush to affirm, "that the laws of the Church do not bind the
conscience, if they are not promulgated by the civil power ; that the
acts and decrees of the Roman Pontiffs concerning religion and the
Church require the sanction and approbation, or at least, the assent of
the civil power ; and that the Apostolic Constitutions, (Clement XII.,
Benedict XIV., Pius VII., Leo XII.) condemning secret societies,
whether these exact or do not exact an oath of secresy, and branding
with anathema their followers and partisans, have no force in those
countries of the world where such associations are tolerated by the
civil Government." It is likewise affirmed, "that the excommunica-
tions launched by the Council of Trent and the Roman Pontiffs against
those who invade and usurp the possessions of the Church and its
rights, strive, by confounding the spiritual and temporal orders, to
attain solely a mere earthly end; that the Church can decide nothing
which may bind the consciences of the faithful in the temporal order
of things ; that the right of the Church is not competent to restrain
with temporal penalties the violators of her laws; and that it is in accordance with the principles of theology and of public law, for the
civil Government to appropriate property possessed by the churches,
the Religious Orders, and other pious establishments." And they
have no shame in avowing openly and publicly the heretical state-

ment and principle, from which have emanated so many errors and perverse opinions, "that the ecclesiastical power is not, by the law of God, made distinct from and independent of the civil power, and that no distinction, no independence of this kind can be maintained without the Church invading and usurping the essential rights of the civil power." Neither can We pass over in silence the audacity of those who, not enduring sound doctrine, assert that "the judgments and decrees of the Holy See, the object of which is declared to concern the general welfare of the Church, its rights, and its discipline, do not claim acquiescence and obedience, under pain of sin and loss of the Catholic profession, if they do not treat of the dogmas of faith and of morals."

How contrary is this doctrine to the Catholic dogma, of the plenary power divinely conferred on the Sovereign Pontiff by Our Lord Jesus Christ, to guide, to supervise and to govern the Universal Church, no one can fail to see and understand, clearly and evidently.

Amid so great a perversity of depraved opinions, We, remembering Our Apostolic duty, and solicitous before all things for Our most holy Religion, for sound doctrine, for the salvation of the souls confided to Us, and for the welfare of human Society itself, have considered the moment opportune to raise anew Our Apostolic voice. Therefore do We, by our Apostolic authority, reprobate, denounce, and condemn generally and particularly all the evil opinions and doctrines specially mentioned in this Letter, and We wish that they may be held as reprobated, denounced and condemned by all the children of the Catholic Church.

But You know further, Venerable Brothers, that in Our time the haters of all truth and justice, and violent enemies of our religion have spread abroad other impious doctrines, by means of pestilent books, pamphlets, and journals, which, distributed over the surface of the earth, deceive the people and wickedly lie. You are not ignorant that in our day men are found who, animated and excited by the spirit of Satan, have arrived at that excess of impiety, as not to fear to deny Our Lord and Master Jesus Christ, and to attack His Divinity with scandalous persistence. And here We cannot abstain from awarding You well-merited praise, Venerable Brothers, for all the care and zeal, with which you have raised Your episcopal voice against so great an impiety.

And therefore in this present letter, We speak to You with all affection; to You who, called to partake Our cares, are Our greatest support in the midst of Our very great grief; Our joy and consolation, by reason of the excellent piety of which You give proof in maintaining religion, and the marvellous love, faith, and discipline with which, united by the strongest and most affectionate ties to Us and this Apostolic See, You strive valiantly and accurately to fulfil Your most weighty episcopal ministry. We do then expect, from Your excellent pastoral zeal, that, taking the sword of the Spirit, which is the Word of God, and strengthened by the grace of Our Lord Jesus Christ, You will watch with redoubled care, that the faithful committed to Your charge "abstain from evil pasturage, which Jesus Christ doth not till, because His Father hath not planted it." (St. Ignatius, M. ad Philadelph. St. Leo, Epist. 156, al. 125). Never cease, then, to inculcate on the faithful that all true happiness for mankind proceeds from our august Religion, from its doctrine and practice, and that that people is happy who have the Lord for their God (Psalm 143). Teach them, "that kingdoms rest upon the foundation of the Catholic faith (St. Celest, Epist., 22 ad Syn. Eph.), and that nothing is so deadly, nothing so certain to engender every ill, nothing so exposed to danger, as for men to believe that they stand in need of nothing else than the free will which we received at birth, if we ask nothing further from the Lord ; that is to say, if forgetting our Author, we abjure His power to show that we are free." And do not omit to teach, "that the royal power has been established, not only to exercise the government of the world, but, above all, for the protection of the Church (St. Leo, Epist. 156 al. 125) ; and that there is nothing more profitable and more glorious for the Sovereigns of States, and Kings, than to leave the Catholic Church to exercise her laws, and not to permit any to curtail her liberty ;" as Our most wise and courageous Predecessor, St. Felix, wrote to the Emperor Zeno. "It is certain that it is advantageous for Sovereigns, when the cause of God is in question, to submit their Royal will, according to his ordinance, to the Priests of Jesus Christ, and not to prefer it before them." (Pius VII. Epist., Encycl., *Diu satis*, 15th May, 1800).

And if always, so especially at present, Venerable Brothers, in the midst of the numerous calamities of the Church and of civil Society, in view also of the terrible conspiracy of our adversaries against the Catholic Church and this Apostolic See, and the great accumulation of errors, it is before all things necessary to go with faith to the Throne of Grace, to obtain mercy and find Grace in timely aid. We have therefore judged it right to excite the piety of all the faithful, in order that, with Us and with You all, they may pray without ceasing to the Father of lights and of mercies, supplicating and beseeching

Him fervently and humbly, and in the plenitude of their faith they may seek refuge in Our Lord Jesus Christ, who has redeemed us to God with His blood, that by their earnest and continual prayers, they may obtain from that most dear Heart, victim of burning charity for us, that it would draw all to Himself by the bonds of His love, that all men being inflamed by His holy love may live according to His heart, pleasing God in all things, and being fruitful in all good works.

But, as there is no doubt that the prayers most agreeable to God, are those of men who approach Him with a heart pure from all stain, We have thought it good to open to Christians, with Apostolic liberality, the heavenly treasures of the Church confided to Our dispensation, so that the faithful, more strongly drawn towards true piety, and purified from the stain of their sins by the Sacrament of Penance, may more confidently offer up their prayers to God and obtain His mercy and grace.

By these Letters therefore, emanating from Our Apostolic authority, We grant to all and each of the faithful of both sexes throughout the Catholic world a Plenary Indulgence, in the manner of a Jubilee, during one month, up to the end of the coming year 1865, and not longer, to be carried into effect by You, Venerable Brethren, and the other legitimate local Ordinaries, in the form and manner laid down at the commencement of Our Sovereign Pontificate by Our Apostolical Letters, in form of a Brief, dated the 20th of November, A. D. 1846, and sent to the whole Episcopate of the world, commencing with the words, "*Arcano Divinæ Providentiæ consilio*," and with the faculties given by Us in those same Letters. We desire, however, that all the prescriptions of Our Letters shall be observed, saving the exceptions We have declared are to be made. And We have granted this, notwithstanding all which might make to the contrary, even those worthy of special and individual mention and derogation; and in order that every doubt and difficulty may be removed, We have ordered that copies of those Letters should be again forwarded to You.

Let us implore, Venerable Brethren, from our inmost hearts, and with all our souls, the mercy of God. He has encouraged us so to do, by saying : "I will not withdraw My mercy from them." "Let us ask and we shall receive ; and if there is slowness or delay in the reception, because we have grievously offended, let us knock, because to him that knocketh it shall be opened ; if our prayers, groans, and tears, in which we must persist and be obstinate, knock at the door : and if our prayers be united ; let each one pray to God, not for himself alone, but for all his brethren, as the Lord hath taught us to pray." (St.

Cyprian, Epistle 11.) But, in order that God may accede more easily to Our and Your prayers, and to those of all His faithful servants, let us employ in all confidence, as our Mediatrix with Him, the Virgin Mary, Mother of God, who "has destroyed all heresies throughout the world, and who, the most loving Mother of us all, is very gracious . . . and full of mercy, ... allows herself to be entreated by all, shows herself most clement towards all, and takes under her pitying care all our necessities with a most ample affection," (*St. Bernard, Serm de duodecim prærogativis B. V. M. in verbis Apocalyp.*); and, "sitting as queen at the right hand of her only begotten Son, Our Lord Jesus Christ, in a golden vestment clothed around with various adornments," there is nothing which she cannot obtain from Him. Let us implore also the intervention of the Blessed Peter, Chief of the Apostles, and of his co-Apostle Paul, and of all those Saints of Heaven, who, having already become the friends of God, have been admitted into the celestial kingdom, where they are crowned and bear palms in their hands; and who, henceforth certain of their own immortality, are sollicitous for our salvation.

In conclusion, We ask of God from Our inmost soul the abundance of all his celestial benefits for You, and We bestow upon You, Venerable Brethren, and upon all the faithful Clergy, and Laity committed to Your care, Our Apostolic Benediction from the most loving depths of Our heart, in token of Our charity toward You.

PIUS, PP. IX.

Given at Rome, from St. Peter's, this 8th day of December, 1864, the tenth anniversary of the Dogmatic Definition of the Immaculate Conception of the Virgin Mary, Mother of God, in the nineteenth year of Our Pontificate.

THE SYLLABUS

Of the Principal Errors of our Time, which are Stigmatized in the Consistorial Allocutions, Encyclical, and other Apostolical Letters of Our Most Holy Father, Pope Pius IX.

Section I.—Pantheism, Naturalism, and Absolute Rationalism.

I. There exists no Divine Power, Supreme Being, Wisdom, and Providence distinct from the universe, and God is none other than nature, and is therefore mutable. In effect, God is produced in man and in the world, and all things are God, and have the very substance of God. God is therefore one and the same thing with the world, and thence spirit is the same thing with matter, necessity with liberty, true with false, good with evil, justice with injustice. (Allocution *Maxima quidem*, 9th June, 1862.)

II. All action of God upon man and the world is to be denied. (Allocution *Maxima quidem*, 9th June, 1862.)

III. Human reason, without any regard to God, is the sole arbiter of truth and falsehood, of good and evil; it is its own law to itself, and suffices by its natural force to secure the welfare of men and of nations. (Allocution *Maxima quidem*, 9th June, 1862.)

IV. All the truths of Religion are derived from the native strength of human reason; whence reason is the master rule by which man can and ought to arrive at the knowledge of all truths of every kind. (Encyclical letters, *Qui pluribus*, 9th November, 1846, *Singulari quidem*, 17th March, 1856, and the Allocution *Maxima quidem*, 9th June, 1862.)

V. Divine revelation is imperfect, and, therefore, subject to a continual and indefinite progress, which corresponds with the progress of human reason. (Encyclical *Qui pluribus*, 9th November, 1846, and the Allocution *Maxima quidem*, 9th June, 1862.)

VI. Christian faith is in opposition to human reason, and divine revelation not only does not benefit, but even injures the perfection of man. (Encyclical *Qui pluribus*, 9th November, 1846, and the Allocution *Maxima quidem*, 9th June, 1862.)

VII. The prophecies and miracles, uttered and narrated in the Sacred Scriptures, are the fictions of poets; and the mysteries of the Christian faith, the result of philosophical investigations. In the books of the two Testaments there are contained mythical inventions, and Jesus Christ is Himself a mythical fiction. (Encyclical *Qui pluribus*, 9th November, 1846, and the Allocution *Maxima quidem*, 9th June, 1862.)

SECTION II.—MODERATE RATIONALISM.

VIII. As human reason is placed on a level with Religion, so theological matters must be treated in the same manner as philosophical ones. (Allocution *Singulari quadem perfusi*, 9th December, 1854.)

IX. All the dogmas of the Christian Religion are, without exception, the object of natural science or philosophy, and human reason, instructed solely by history, is able, by its own natural strength and principles, to arrive at the true knowledge of even the most abstruse dogmas; *provided* such dogmas be proposed as subject matter for human reason. (Letter to the Archbishop Frising. *Gravissimas*, 11th December, 1862—to the same, *Tuas libenter*, 21st December, 1863.)

X. As the philosopher is one thing, and philosophy is another, so it is the right and duty of the philosopher to submit himself to the authority which he shall have recognised as true; but philosophy neither can nor ought to submit to any authority. (Letter to Archbishop Frising. Gravissimas, 11th December, 1862—to the same, *Tuas libenter*, 21st December, 1863.)

XI. The Church not only ought never to animadvert upon philosophy, but ought to tolerate the errors of philosophy, leaving to philosophy the care of their correction. (Letter to Archbishop Frising. 11th December, 1862.)

XII. The decrees of the Apostolic See and of the Roman Congregation fetter the free progress of science. (Id. Ibid.)

XIII. The method and principles, by which the old scholastic Doctors cultivated theology, are no longer suitable to the demands of the age and the progress of science. (Ib. Tuas libenter, 21st December, 1863.)

XIV. Philosophy must be treated of without any account being taken of supernatural revelation. (Id. Ibid.)

N. B.—To the rationalistic system belong, in great part, the errors of Anthony Gunther, condemned in the letter to the Cardinal Archbishop of Cologne "*Eximiam tuam*," June 15, 1847; and in that to the Bishop of Breslau, "*Dolore haud mediocri*," April 30, 1860.)

Section III.—Indifferentism, Latitudinarianism.

XV. Every man is free to embrace and profess the Religion he shall believe true, guided by the light of reason. (Apostolic Letters Multiplices inter, 10th June 1851. Allocution Maxima quidem, 9th June 1862.)

XVI. Men may in any religion find the way of eternal salvation, and obtain eternal salvation. (Encyclical letter Qui pluribus, 9th November, 1846. Allocution, Ubi primum, 17th December, 1847. Encyclical letter Singulari quidem, 17th March, 1856.)

XVII. We may entertain at least a well-founded hope for the eternal salvation of all those, who are in no manner in the true Church of Christ. (Allocution Singulari quadem, 9th December, 1854. Encyclical letter Quanto conficiamur, 17th August, 1863.)

XVIII. Protestantism is nothing more than another form of the same true Christian Religion, in which it is possible to be equally pleasing to God as in the Catholic Church. (Encyclical letter Noscitis et nobiscum, 8th December, 1849.)

Section IV.—Socialism, Communism, Secret Societies, Birlical Societies, Clerico-Liberal Societies.

Pests of this description are frequently rebuked in the severest terms in the Encyc. *Qui pluribus,* Nov. 9, 1846; Alloc. *Quibus quantisque,* Aug. 20, 1849; Encyc. *Nescitis et Nobiscum,* Dec. 8, 1849; Alloc. *Singulari quadam,* Dec. 8, 1854; Encyc. *Quanto conficiamur mœrore,"* Aug. 10, 1863.

Section V.—Errors Concerning the Church and Her Rights.

XIX. The Church is not a true, and perfect, and entirely free society, nor does she enjoy peculiar and perpetual rights conferred upon her by her Divine Founder, but it appertains to the civil power to define, what are the rights and limits within which the Church may exercise authority. (Allocution Singulari quadem, 9th December, 1854, Multis gravibusque, 17th December, 1860, Maxima quidem, 9th June, 1862.)

XX. The ecclesiastical power must not exercise its authority without the permission and assent of the civil Government. (Allocution; Meminit unusquisque, 30th September, 1861.)

XX1. The Church has not the power of defining dogmatically, that the Religion of the Catholic Church is the only true Religion. (Apostolic Letters Multiplices inter, 10th June, 1851.)

XXII. The obligation which binds Catholic teachers and authors applies only to those things, which are proposed for universal belief as dogmas of the faith, by the infallible judgment of the Church. (Letters to Archbishop Frising. Tuas libenter, 21st Dec., 1863.)

XXIII. The Roman Pontiffs and Œcumenical Councils have exceeded the limits of their power, have usurped the rights of Princes, and have even committed errors in defining matters of faith and morals. (Apost. Letter, Multiplices inter, 10th June 1851.)

XXIV. The Church has not the power of availing herself of force, or any direct or indirect temporal power. (Letter Apost. Ad. Apostolicæ, 22nd Aug., 1851.)

XXV. In addition to the authority inherent in the Episcopate, a further and temporal power is granted to it by the civil authority, either expressly or tacitly, which power is on that account also revocable by the civil authority whenever it pleases. (Letter Apost. Ad. Apostolicæ, 22nd Aug., 1851.)

XXVI. The Church has not the innate and legitimate right of acquisition and possession. (Allocution Nunquam fore, 18th Dec., 1856. Encyclical Incredibili, 17th Sept., 1863.)

XXVII. The ministers of the Church and the Roman Pontiff ought to be absolutely excluded from all charge and dominion over temporal affairs. (Allocution Maxima quidem, 9th June, 1862.)

XXVIII. Bishops have not the right of promulgating even their Apostolical letters, without the permission of the Government. (Allocution Nunquam fore, 15th December, 1856.)

XXIX. Dispensations granted by the Roman Pontiff must be considered null, unless they have been asked for by the civil Government. (Id. Ibid.)

XXX. The immunity of the Church and of ecclesiastical persons derives its origin from civil law. (Apost. Multiplices inter, 10th June, 1851.)

XXXI. Ecclesiastical *Courts* for the temporal causes, of the clergy, whether civil or criminal, ought by all means to be abolished, even without the concurrence and against the protest of the Holy See. (Allocution Acerbissimum, 27th September, 1852. And. Nunquam fore, 15th December, 1856.)

XXXII. The personal immunity exonerating the clergy from military service may be abolished, without violation either of natural right or of equity. Its abolition is called for by civil progress, especially in a community constituted upon principles of Liberal Government. (Letter to the Archbishop of Montreal, Singularis nobisque, 29th September, 1864.)

XXXIII. It does not appertain exclusively to ecclesiastical jurisdiction, by any right proper and inherent, to direct the teaching of theological subjects. (Letter to Archbishop Frising. Tuas libenter, 21st December, 1863.)

XXXIV. The teaching of those, who compare the Sovereign Pontiff to a free Sovereign acting in the Universal Church, is a doctrine which prevailed in the Middle Ages. (Letter Apost. Ad. Apostolicæ, 22nd August, 1851.)

XXXV. There would be no obstacle to the sentence of a General Council, or the act of all the universal peoples, transferring the Pontifical Sovereignty from the Bishop and city of Rome to some other bishopric and some other city. (Id. Ibid.)

XXXVI. The definition of a National Council does not admit of any subsequent discussion, and the civil power can regard as settled an affair decided by such National Council. (Id. Ibid.)

XXXVII. National Churches can be established, after being withdrawn and plainly separated from the authority of the Roman Pontiff. (Allocution Multis gravibusque, 17th December, 1860. Jamdudum cernimus, 18th March, 1861.)

XXXVIII. Roman Pontiffs have, by their too arbitray conduct, contributed to the division of the Church into Eastern and Western. (Letter Apost. Ad. Apostolicæ, 22nd August, 1851.)

SECTION VI.—ERRORS ABOUT CIVIL SOCIETY, CONSIDERED BOTH IN ITSELF AND IN ITS RELATION TO THE CHURCH.

XXXIX. The Republic is the origin and source of all rights, and possesses rights which are not circumscribed by any limits. (Allocution Maxima quidem, 9th June, 1862.)

XL. The teaching of the Catholic Church is opposed to the well-being and interests of society. (Encyclical Qui pluribus, 9th November, 1846, Allocution Quibus quantisque, 20th April, 1849.)

XLI. The Civil power, even when exercised by an infidel Sovereign, possesses an indirect and negative power over religious affairs. It, therefore, possesses not only the right called that of *exequatur*, but that of the (so-called) *appellatio ab abusu.** (Apostolic Letter, Ad. 22d August, 1851.)

XLII. In the case of conflicting laws between the two Powers, the civil law ought to prevail. (Letter Apost. Ad. Apostolicæ, 22nd August, 1851.)

* The power of authorising official acts of the Papal power, and of correcting the alleged abuses of the same.

XLIII. The civil power has a right to break, and to declare and render null the conventions (commonly called Concordats), concluded with the Apostolic See, relative to the use of rights appertaining to the ecclesiastical immunity, without the consent of the Holy See, and even contrary to its protest. (Allocution In consistoriali, 1st November, 1850. Multis gravibusque, 17th December, 1861.)

XLIV. The civil authority may interfere in matters relating to Religion, morality, and spiritual government. Hence it has control over the instructions for the guidance of consciences issued, conformably with their mission, by the Pastors of the Church. Further it possesses power to decree, in the matter of administering the divine Sacraments, as to the dispositions necessary for their reception. (Allocution In Consistoriali, 1st November, 1850. Allocution Maxima quidem, 9th June, 1862.)

XLV. The entire direction of public schools, in which the youth of Christian States are educated, except (to a certain extent) in the case of Episcopal Seminaries, may and must appertain to the civil power, and belong to it so far, that no other authority whatsoever shall be recognized as having any right to interfere in the discipline of the schools, the arrangement of the studies, the taking of degrees, or the choice and approval of the teachers.—(Allocution in Consistoriali, 1st November, 1850.—Allocution Quibus luctuosissimis, 5th September, 1851.)

XLVI. Much more, even in Clerical Seminaries, the method of study to be adopted is subject to the civil authority. (Allocution Nunquam fore, 15th December, 1856.)

XLVII. The best theory of civil society requires, that popular schools open to the children of all classes, and, generally, all public institutes intended for instruction in letters and philosophy, and for conducting the education of the young, should be freed from all ecclesiastical authority, government, and interference, and should be fully subjected to the civil and political power, in conformity with the will of rulers and the prevalent opinions of the age. (Letter to the Archbishop of Fribourg, Quam non sine, 14th July, 1864.)

XLVIII. This system of instructing youth, which consists in separating it from the Catholic faith and from the power of the Church, and in teaching exclusively, or at least primarily, the knowledge of natural things and the earthly ends of social life alone, may be approved by Catholics. (Id. Ibid.)

XLIX. The civil power has the right to prevent ministers of Religion, and the faithful, from communicating freely and mutually with each other, and with the Roman Pontiff. (Allocution Maxima qudem, 9th June, 1862.)

L. The secular authority possesses, as inherent in itself, the right of presenting Bishops, and may require of them that they take possession of their dioceses, before having received canonical institution and the Apostolical letters from the Holy See. (Allocution Nunquam fore, 15th December, 1856.)

LI. And further, the Secular Government has the right of deposing Bishops from their Pastoral functions, and it is not bound to obey the Roman Pontiff, in those things which relate to Episcopal Sees and the institution of Bishops. (Letter Apost. Multiplices inter 10th June, 1851. Allocution, Acerbissimum, 28th Sept., 1852.)

LII. The Government has of itself the right to alter the age prescribed by the Church for the religious profession, both of men and women ; and it may enjoin upon all religious establishments, to admit no person to take solemn vows without its permission. (Allocution Nunquam fore, 15th Dec., 1856.)

LIII. The laws for the protection of religious establishments, and securing their rights and duties, ought to be abolished: nay more, the civil government may lend its assistance to all who desire to quit the religious life they have undertaken, and break their vows. The government may also suppress Religious Orders, collegiate Churches, and simple Benefices, even those belonging to private patronage, and submit their goods and revenues to the administration and disposal of the civil power. (Allocution Acerbissimum, 27th Sept., 1852. Allocution, Probe memineritis, 22nd January, 1855. Allocution, Cum sæpe, 26th July, 1855.)

LIV. Kings and princes are not only exempt from the jurisdiction of the Church, but are superior to the Church, in litigated questions of jurisdiction. (Letter Apost. Multiplices inter, 10th June, 1851.)

LV. The Church ought to be separated from the State, and the State from the Church. (Allocution Acerbissimum, 27th September, 1852.)

SECTION VII.—ERRORS CONCERNING NATURAL AND CHRISTIAN ETHICS.

LVI. Moral laws do not stand in need of the divine sanction, and there is no necessity that human laws should be conformable to the law of nature, and receive their sanction from God. (Allocution Maxima quidem, 9th June, 1862.)

LVII. Knowledge of philosophical things and morals, and also civil laws may and must be independent of divine and ecclesiastical authority. (Allocution Maxima quidem, 9th June, 1862.)

LVIII. No other forces are to be recognized than those which reside in matter, and all moral teaching and moral excellence ought to be made to consist in the accumulation and increase of riches by every possible means, and in the enjoyment of pleasure. (Allocution Maxima quidem, 9th June, 1862. Encyclical Quanto conficiamur, 10th August, 1863.)

LIX. Right consists in the material fact, and all human duties are but vain words, and all human acts have the force of right. (Allocution Maxima quidem, 9th June, 1862.)

LX. Authority is nothing else, but the result of numerical superiority and material force. (Allocution Maxima quidem,. 9th June, 1862.)

LXI. An unjust act, being successful, inflicts no injury upon the sanctity of right. (Allocution Jamdudum cernimus, 18th March, 1861.)

LXII. The principle of *non-intervention*, as it is called, ought to be proclaimed and adhered to. (Allocution Novos et ante, 28th September, 1860.)

LXIII. It is allowable to refuse obedience to legitimate Princes ; nay more, to rise in insurrection against them. (Encyclical Qui pluribus, 9th November, 1846. Allocution Quisque vestrum, 4th October, 1847. Encyclical Noscitis et nobiscum, 8th December, 1849. Letter Apostolicæ Cum Catholica, 26th March, 1860.)

LXIV. The violation of a solemn oath, even every wicked and flagitious action repugnant to the eternal law, is not only not blameable, but quite lawful, and worthy of the highest praise, when done for the love of country. (Allocution Quibus quantisque, 20th April, 1849.)

SECTION VIII.—ERRORS CONCERNING CHRISTIAN MARRIAGE.

LXV. It cannot be by any means tolerated, to maintain that Christ has raised marriage to the dignity of a sacrament. (Apostolical Letter Ad Apostolicæ, 22d August, 1851.)

LXVI. The sacrament of marriage is only an adjunct of the contract, and separable from it, and the sacrament itself consists in the nuptial benediction alone. (Id. ibid.)

LXVII. By the law of nature, the marriage tie is not indissoluble, and in many cases divorce, properly so called, may be pronounced by the civil authority. (Id. ibid.; Allocution Acerbissimum, 27th September, 1852.)

LXVIII. The Church has not the power of laying down what are diriment impediments to marriage. The civil authority does possess such a power, and can do away with existing impediments to marriage. (Let. Apost. Multiplices inter, 10th June, 1851.)

LXIX. The Church only commenced in later ages to bring in diriment impediments, and then availing herself of a right not her own, but borrowed from the civil power. (Let. Apost. Ad Apostolicæ, 22d August, 1851.)

LXX. The canons of the Council of Trent, which pronounce censure of anathema against those who deny to the Church the right of laying down what are diriment impediments, either are not dogmatic, or must be understood as referring only to such borrowed power. (Let. Apost. ibid.)

LXXI. The form of solemnizing marriage prescribed by the said Council, under penalty of nullity, does not bind in cases where the civil law has appointed another form, and where it decrees that this new form shall effectuate a valid marriage. (Id. ibid.)

LXXII. Boniface VIII. is the first who declared, that the vow of chastity pronounced at Ordination annuls nuptials. (Id. ibid.)

LXXIII. A merely civil contract may, among Christians, constitute a true marriage, and it is false, either that the marriage contract between Christians is always a sacrament, or that the contract is null if the sacrament be excluded. (Id. ibid., Letter to King of Sardinia, 9th September, 1852. Allocution Acerbissimum, 27th September, 1852; Multis gravibusque, 17th December, 1860.)

LXXIV. Matrimonial causes and espousals belong by their very nature to civil jurisdiction. (Let. Apost., 22d August, 1851. Allocution Acerbissimum, 27th September, 1859.)

N. B. Two other errors may tend in this direction, those upon the abolition of the celibacy of Priests, and the preference due to the state of marriage over that of virginity. These have been proscribed; the first in the Encyclical "*Qui pluribus*," Nov. 9, 1846; the second in the Letters Apostolical "*Multiplices inter*," June 10, 1851.

SECTION IX.—ERRORS REGARDING THE CIVIL POWER OF THE SOVEREIGN PONTIFF.

LXXV. The children of the Christian and Catholic Church are not agreed upon the compatibility of the temporal with the spiritual power. (Let. Apost. Ad Apostolicæ, 22d August 1851.)

43

LXXVI. The abolition of the temporal power, of which the Apostolic See is possessed, would contribute in the greatest degree to the liberty and prosperity of the Church. (Al. Quibus quantisque, 20th April, 1849.)

N.B. Besides these errors, explicitly noted, many others are impliedly rebuked by the proposed and asserted doctrine, which all Catholics are bound most firmly to hold, touching the temporal Sovereignty of the Roman Pontiff. These doctrines are clearly stated in the Allocutions "Quibus quantisque," April 20, 1859, and "*Si semper antea*," May 20, 1850; Letters Apost. "*Quum Catholica Ecclesia*," March 26, 1860; Allocutions "*Novas*," Sept. 28, 1860; "*Jamdudum*," March 18, 1861, and "*Maxima quidem*," June 9, 1862.

SECTION X.—ERRORS HAVING REFERENCE TO MODERN LIBERALISM.

LXXVII. In the present day, it is no longer expedient that the Catholic Religion shall be held as the only Religion of the State, to the exclusion of all other modes of Worship. (Allocution Nemo vestrum, 26th July, 1855.)

LXXVIII. Whence it has been wisely provided by law, in some countries called Catholic, that persons coming to reside therein shall enjoy the public exercise of their own worship. (Allocution Acerbissimum, 27th September, 1852.)

LXXIX. Moreover it is false, that the civil liberty of every mode of worship, and the full power given to all of overtly and publicly manifesting their opinions and their ideas, of all kinds whatsoever, conduce more easily to corrupt the morals and minds of the people, and to the propagation of the pest of indifferentism. (Allocution Nunquam fore, 15th December, 1856.)

LXXX. The Roman Pontiff can, and ought, to reconcile himself to, and agree with progress, liberalism, and civilization as lately introduced. (Allocution Jamdudum cernimus, 18th March, 1861.)

www.ingramcontent.com/pod-product-compliance
Lightning Source LLC
Chambersburg PA
CBHW061236260626
47172CB00003B/885